Other titles in the same series

Ghost Goalie
The Tigers football team are full of confidence about the next match. But their coach falls ill just before they are due to play! The Tigers are desperate. How can they win without him? Perhaps they can, with a very special bit of ghostly help . . .

Save the Pitch
It's the crucial last game of the season and the Tigers football team must win to go to the top of the League. But the pitch has been invaded by workmen laying new pipes, and it looks like the game will be called off. Can the Tigers get help – fast?

The Terrible Trainer
The Tigers football team have a substitute coach, but he is mean and shouts a lot. He makes the Tigers feel awful. How can they get rid of Mr Bawl and find a coach who will make sure they can win?

The Cup Final
The Tigers football team have to win this last game to win the Cup! But disaster strikes when their coach's head becomes stuck in some iron railings when trying to get the ball. What can they do to save the match?

Ghost Striker
The Tigers football team are facing a difficult away match against a tough team, but they have got the special help of their ghost goalie . . . or have they? Things look bad when an old opponent arrives – intent on revenge!

Tigers on Television

J. BURCHETT AND S. VOGLER

ILLUSTRATED by Guy Parker-Rees

BLOOMSBURY

LONDON BERLIN NEW YORK

Bloomsbury Publishing, London, Berlin and New York

First published in Great Britain in 1999 by Bloomsbury Publishing Plc
36 Soho Square, London, W1D 3QY
This edition published in July 2010

Text copyright © Janet Burchett and Sara Vogler 1999
Illustrations copyright © Guy Parker-Rees 1999
The moral rights of the author and illustrator have been asserted

A CIP catalogue record of this book is available from the British Library

ISBN 978 1 4088 0831 3

FSC
Mixed Sources
Product group from well-managed
forests and other controlled sources
Cert no. SGS-COC-2061
www.fsc.org
© 1996 Forest Stewardship Council

Printed in Great Britain by Clays Ltd, St Ives plc, Bungay, Suffolk

1 3 5 7 9 10 8 6 4 2

www.bloomsbury.com/childrens

Tigers on Television

It was Saturday morning. Billy Bright and the Tigers Under-Tens Football Team were warming up in Tottingham Town park. They had a league match against Crystal Rovers. Their coach, Billy's dad, was pacing up and down the touchline, looking at his watch.

'What's up, Mr Bright?' asked Mona the goalkeeper.

'Nervous about the match?' said Bullseye.

'We beat the Rovers last time,' said Kim.

'*And* Blocker had his boots on the wrong feet,' added Lisa.

'I'm not worried,' said Billy's dad. 'I've got something exciting to tell you. The Tigers are going to be on television!'

'You're joking!' gasped Terry.

'I don't believe you, Dad!' said Billy.

'I'll prove it,' said Mr Bright. 'I've got a letter.'

He marched over to his car and

rummaged around on the back seat.

'Here it is,' he said. He slammed the car door shut.

Billy read the letter out.

C.T.V.

16 OCTOBER

Dear Mr. Bright,

As arranged, Chloe Small and the camera crew will be coming to film the Tigers for "Whiz kids!" this Saturday.

Yours sincerely,

Pru Juicer

'*Whiz Kids!*' yelled Rick. 'That's my favourite programme!'

'Chloe Small!' gasped Ellen. 'She's brilliant!'

'We're going to be famous!' shouted Joe.

'Calm down!' said Dad.

'Why didn't you tell us before?' asked Billy.

'Because *Whiz Kids!* want to film you doing what you do best – playing good football,' explained Dad. 'You might have got a bit carried away if you'd known earlier. They'll be here any minute. Let's get on with the practice.'

The Tigers dashed back towards the pitch. Mr Bright went to follow. There was a ripping sound. Dad stood still.

'Come on, Dad,' called Billy.

'I can't!' wailed Mr Bright.

'He's got stage fright!' laughed Rob.

'No!' yelled Mr Bright. 'I'm stuck.'

Billy ran back to the car. Dad's tracksuit trousers were caught in the door.

'Open the door,' said Billy.

'I locked it!' said Dad.

'Where are the keys then?' asked Billy.

'In there,' said Dad miserably.

The car keys were sitting on the front seat.

'You could climb out of your trousers, Mr Bright,' suggested Kim.

'Yes, I could,' said Billy's
dad. He thought for a moment.
'No, I can't.'

Mr Bright whispered to Billy.
Billy whispered to the team.
The Tigers giggled.

'Your mum will be along later,' said Billy's dad gloomily. 'I hope she's got her spare keys.'

A van drove through the park gates and came slowly towards them. It said CTV on the side.

'Chloe Small's here!' wailed Blocker.

'We're going to look really stupid,' said Ellen.

'We're hopeless without a coach,' said Rob.

'Billy will coach us,' said Joe. 'Won't you, Billy?'

Billy nodded. Dad was a bit accident prone so Billy often took over as coach. The Tigers thought he used a coaching book. But Billy didn't have a book. He had Springer Spannell, Tottingham Town's most famous goalkeeper, to help him.

No one else knew that when Billy coached, Springer was on the touchline. No one else could see Springer. Springer Spannell was . . . a ghost! And Billy had to keep him a secret. It was in Springer's PhIFA rules.

Billy was a hopeless coach on his own. And he didn't want to look silly in front of the TV

camera. But there was no sign of the ghost goalie and Chloe Small was coming over. The Tigers gawped in admiration. Dad's face went red.

'Mr Bright?' said Chloe Small. 'Nice to meet you. Shall we get started?'

'Dad can't coach,' explained Billy. 'He's got . . .'

'. . . a brilliant idea!' burst in Mr Bright. 'Billy will coach the Tigers.'

'Super!' said Chloe. 'That's what *Whiz Kids!* is all about. Kids doing it for themselves. Now Billy, let's see the Tigers in practice.'

'Well . . .' said Billy.

'No need to be shy,' laughed

Chloe. 'You'll soon forget the camera is there. Just be careful not to trip over the cables. Now, what are you going to do first?'

The Tigers looked at Billy. Billy looked round for Springer.

'Er . . .' said Billy. 'I'll let
the team choose.'

'Super!' said Chloe Small.

'Right then,' said Billy,
nervously. 'Who's going
first?'

The team ran on to the pitch.

They all wanted to be on camera at once.

'What's this?' said a voice. 'Looks like a horror film.'

Billy looked up. A man was standing on the touchline. He was wobbly round the edges and Billy could see right through him. It was like looking through a cucumber jelly. It was Springer!

'Sorry I'm late,' said Springer. 'I got diverted by the road-works at the roundabout. Where's your dad this time?'

Billy told him.

'Oh dear,' chuckled Springer. 'Tell him not to wriggle. Now, what's going on here?'

Billy showed Springer the letter.

Blocker's famous Egyptian sand dance

'Great!' said Springer. 'I was on telly once. It was black and white in those days. Wonder what I'll look like in colour.'

'No!' yelled Billy. 'They might film you! You mustn't be seen.'

The cameraman didn't bat an

eyelid, but Chloe Small looked puzzled.

'I have to be seen!' she said. 'I present the programme.'

Billy heaved a sigh of relief. No one could see the ghost goalie.

'I think the Tigers are rather

...ses are red, footballs are brown,
...played in Goal for Tottingham Town.

excited,' Chloe Small went on. 'Shall we try again? I'm sure you'll want the viewers to see you at your best.'

'Great idea!' said Billy. 'They'll play well now Springer's here.'

He led the Tigers on to the pitch.

'Let's show them how to do it properly,' called Springer from the touchline. 'Dribbling and tackling – in pairs.'

When Crystal Rovers arrived, Chloe Small called the Tigers over.

'That practice was super!' she said. 'Now we'll film some of the action. Good luck, Tigers!'

Billy couldn't wait to see the finished *Whiz Kids!* programme. With Springer's secret coaching, nothing could go wrong. The Tigers would be famous.

The Rovers won the toss and chose ends. The cameraman raised his camera to his shoulder. The sound man lifted

his fluffy microphone. The referee blew his whistle and Bullseye kicked off.

The Rovers had some new players, and the Tigers soon realised it would be a tough game.

Bullseye tapped the ball to Billy, who pushed it out to the

wing, where Rick picked it up. A Rovers' midfielder moved in straight away and took possession. Play came into the Tigers' half.

'Come on, Tigers!' shouted Springer. 'Launch a counter-attack! Tell Terry to block that striker till the others get there.'

'Terry, block him!' shouted Billy. 'Blocker and Lisa – get up in support!'

But the Rovers' striker dodged Terry and headed for goal. Blocker and Lisa sprinted after him. Springer dashed up the touchline. The camera crew followed the action. Mona was ready on her toes in the goal mouth. The striker belted the

ball at the goal. Mona sprang
in the air and punched it away.
The striker caught it on the
volley and hammered the ball
at the net again. It looked like
a certain goal. But with a
perfectly judged dive, Mona

gathered the ball safely to her chest.

'Brilliant save, Mona!' yelled Springer. 'I hope they got it on film.'

'Super!' said Chloe Small to the cameraman. 'I hope you

SMASH

got it on film.'

'I'll rewind and check,' said the cameraman.

Mona was getting ready to kick the ball up the pitch.

'Now Tigers,' called Springer, 'fast on your feet. One touch passing. Don't give the ball away.'

'One touch passing,' Billy called to the Tigers. 'Don't give the ball away.'

Joe received the ball from Mona and knocked it straight on to Lisa.

'Over to Rob!' shouted Springer.

'To Rob!' shouted Billy.

With a long, low pass, Lisa sent the ball to Rob.

'Perfect!' yelled Springer, running along the touchline. 'Lob it to B . . .' Suddenly, Springer stopped dead.

Billy looked over.

'Lob it to who?' he called.

'I dunno!' said Blocker.

'Not you, Blocker,' sighed Billy.

'Bottibol!' shouted Springer.

'Botty's ball?' repeated Billy, scratching his head.

'Who's Botty?' said Kim.

'It can't be Billy!' laughed Ellen. 'He's *potty*!'

The Rovers had gained possession. But Billy didn't notice. He was watching

Springer. The ghost goalie was dashing along the touchline – backwards.

'Stop messing about, Springer!' hissed Billy, running after him.

But Springer didn't seem to hear him. He stopped and then ran forwards again. But this time he did it all in slow motion. Billy stood and watched in amazement. He didn't notice he was standing in the Tigers' goal area.

'The filming is looking fine, Chloe,' called the cameraman.

He stopped the playback and Springer came to a halt. The ghost goalie looked puzzled.

'This is our big moment,' said

Billy to Springer, 'and you're just showing off.'

'No, I'm not,' said Blocker, as he ran past. 'I'm saving my famous handspring for the second half.'

'Not you, Blocker,' sighed Billy.

'Sorry, Billy,' called Springer. 'I don't know what came over me.' He looked at the game. 'Quick,' he said, 'mind the ball!'

'Quick, Billy,' yelled Ellen, 'mind the ball!'

But it was too late. The Rovers' striker had blasted the ball at goal. The shot was wide. Well, it would have been wide, if the ball hadn't bounced off the back of Billy's head and

straight into the goal. The
Rovers were one-nil up.

The cameraman was shaking
his head.

'We were told they were a
good team,' said Chloe Small.
'We may have to look
elsewhere.'

Billy felt dreadful. He had scored an own goal – in front of the cameras!

'Sorry, everyone,' he murmured.

By half-time the Tigers were two-nil down. They slouched off the pitch.

'I don't know what's got into Billy,' said Lisa.

'He kept yelling at thin air,' complained Kim.

'He shouted 'elbbird' at me,' moaned Joe. 'He said it's in his coaching book.'

'Birdwatching book, more

like,' said Blocker.

Chloe Small came over.

'I've never seen coaching like that,' she said, trying to smile. 'Perhaps your dad could take over now.'

Billy looked over to the car-park. Dad was still stuck to the car and there was no sign of Mum.

'He can't,' said Billy. 'It's his pants . . . I mean, it makes him pant!'

'Oh dear,' said Chloe Small. 'Tell him he needs to get fit!'

Billy didn't know what to do. Springer had gone mad and the Tigers were losing the chance to be on *Whiz Kids!* Then he overheard the cameraman and the sound man. They were fiddling with the camera.

'It's the latest model,' the

cameraman was saying. 'Let me show you what it can do.'

The sound man peered through the viewfinder. The cameraman flicked a switch.

'The wobble,' he said.

Billy suddenly saw Springer wobbling like a plate of jelly. The cameraman twisted a dial.

'The shrink.'

Springer stopped wobbling

and shrank to the size of a
football.

'The split screen,' said the
cameraman, as he pressed a
button.

Springer grew back to his
normal size, then his legs went
left and the rest of his body
went right. Billy gawped. Then
he realised what was going on.

'It's the camera!' yelled Billy.

''Course it is, son,' said the

cameraman. 'What did you
think it was?'

Billy ran over to the top half
of Springer.

'It's the camera doing this to
you!' he whispered. 'You've got
to get out of its range. The
moment you get your legs
back, run away!'

'Thanks, Billy!' said Springer, weakly. 'I was beginning to think I had phantom flu. There's nothing about this in my PhIFA rules.'

As soon as Springer found his legs, he sprinted away across the park. But at that moment, the cameraman

decided to rewind the film.
Springer came back again.

There's only one thing for it,
thought Billy. If the Tigers were

going to show Chloe Small how
good they really were, he'd
have to stop the camera
somehow, so that Springer

could escape. He walked
around, thinking hard.

All of a sudden, Billy found
himself flat on his face. He had

tripped over the camera cable.
He sat up and rubbed his knee.
Then he realised that he had
pulled the lead out of the

camera with his foot. This was the chance Springer needed.

'Quick, Springer!' he hissed. 'Run away.'

Springer fled. The cameraman scowled at Billy. He plugged the camera back in and carried on rewinding. But Springer had reached the other side of the park. He was safe.

The teams took their positions for the second half. The Rovers kicked off, but Lisa won the ball with a brilliant tackle. She tapped the ball to Bullseye. Bullseye lobbed it over to Rick. Rick was tightly marked. Billy waited for Springer's instructions. Then he realised

that Springer could be chanting his eleven times table for all he knew. He couldn't hear a word. It was going to be a disaster. The Tigers were going to lose. And the only television programme they would get on was 'How *Not* To Play Football'.

Then suddenly, he heard a booming voice.

'TESTING, TESTING, ONE, TWO, THREE. SPRINGER CALLING. CAN YOU HEAR ME, BILLY? WAVE YOUR ARMS IF YOU CAN.'

Billy jumped in the air with a whoop and waved his arms. Rick was so surprised he kicked the ball out of play.

'Being on television's gone to Billy's brain,' muttered Lisa.

'I wish this was over,' wailed Ellen.

'I wish I could go home,' said Bullseye.

'I CAN COACH YOU FROM HERE, BILLY!' called Springer.

'I EXPECT YOU ARE WONDERING HOW I AM DOING THIS,' called Springer. 'PhIFA RULE NUMBER FOURTEEN. IF A GHOST COACH HAS TO COACH FROM A DISTANCE, HE

MAY USE A GHOST
LOUDSPEAKER AND
BINOCULARS. NOW LET'S
GET THIS SHOW ON THE
ROAD.'

The Rovers got ready to take
the throw. Billy called to his
team.

'Sorry about that, Tigers. I
was . . . a bit camera shy. I'm
all right now. There's still time
to win.'

As the ball sailed into play,
Billy leapt and intercepted it
with a header. It went straight
to Blocker's feet. He curled the
ball over to Rick. Rick pushed
it to Bullseye, who lobbed it to
Kim. Kim found herself

surrounded by defenders and backheeled the ball to Rob.

'HAVE A SHOT, ROB!' yelled Springer.

'Shoot, Rob!' screeched Billy. Rob drilled the ball into the back of the net. On the other side of the park, Springer leapt in the air. At last, the Tigers were playing like the good football team they were.

The cameraman kept his film rolling.

'Super!' sighed Chloe Small. 'This will be the best *Whiz Kids!* ever.' She quickly combed her hair and grabbed the microphone. 'The Tigers are playing like a Premiership side. It's action like this that has

made them the good team they
are. Now Ellen has the ball.
She's passed to Terry. On to
Joe. It's a brilliant punt across
to Lisa. She's tapped it to Kim.
Kim to Billy. Billy's not going
to shoot from there, is he? It's
an awkward angle . . . he has!
It's skimmed the post . . . and
it's a goal!'

'DO IT AGAIN!' shouted Springer.

'Do it again!' shouted the Tigers' supporters.

Soon the Tigers were back in the Rovers' goal mouth. Bullseye blasted the ball at goal, but the Rovers' keeper pushed it round the post. It was

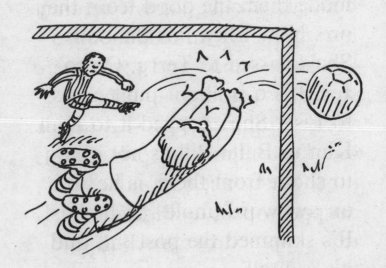

a Tigers' corner. Billy placed
the ball by the corner flag and
took three steps back.

'HIT IT TO THE NEAR
POST!' shouted Springer.

Billy hit the ball with the side
of his boot. The ball curled
through the air. Tigers and
Rovers leapt up to meet it. A
Rovers' defender headed the
ball out. Blocker saw it coming
his way. This was the moment
for Chloe Small and the camera
to see his famous handspring.
Blocker jumped on to his hands
and kicked his legs up behind
him. The goalie's mouth
dropped open, as Blocker's
flying heels drove the ball into
the back of the net. It was

three-two. The Tigers were in
the lead.

Over in the car-park, Billy's
mum sorted out her keys and
unlocked the car.

'Thanks, love,' said Mr
Bright. 'Now I can take over

the coaching. I'll be on
television after all!'
    He arrived at the touchline
just as the final whistle blew.

Three weeks later, the Tigers
were on television.